DOGGY HAIR!

© 2013 Bobbi Evenson, Founder for Buster's Vision Nonprofit, Inc. (501c3 Organization)
Illustrations by: Jesse Mincin

1st Edition
ISBN: 978-0-578-11759-1, CPSIA: 4-2013 M10862 (Softcover)
ISBN: 978-0-9891678-0-2, CPSIA: 3-2013 D12241 (Hardcover)
ISBN: 978-0-9891678-1-9 (ePub)
ISBN: 978-0-9891678-3-3 (mobi)
US Copyright Registration Number: TXu 1-848-380

Created in the United States by BookMasters, Inc.
30 Amberwood Parkway, Ashland, OH 44805

Learn more about Buster's Vision at http://bustersvision.com or follow us via our
Multi-Media Social Network: LinkedIn, Facebook, Twitter, Pinterest, Instagram, or YouTube.
(Widgets are located at Buster's Vision Nonprofit's website.)

Positive, Encouraging, Buster's Vision!
ONE VOICE CAN MAKE A DIFFERENCE!

Thank you for your contribution.
Proceeds go to Buster's Vision Nonprofit, Inc.
501c3 Organization
http://bustersvision.com

**In Loving Memory of my parents, Jack & Jean Evenson,
who rescued many abandoned animals from the
Minnesota and Dakota Prairies.**

DOGGY HAIR!

Written by Bobbi Evenson

Illustrated by Jesse Mincin

Hair! Hair! Hair!
Hair on the carpet! Hair on the steps!
Hair on the furniture! Oh what a mess!
That Hair! That Hair! It covers my dress!
That Hair! That Hair! Oh what a mess!
That Hair! That Hair! It's everywhere!

Hair! Hair! Hair!
Oh my! Oh my!
That Hair! That Hair! It's everywhere!
Golly! Golly! What do I do?
That Hair! That Hair! It's everywhere!

Hair! Hair! Hair!
Mommy vacuums the carpet. Daddy sweeps all the floors.
Mommy vacuums my dress. Daddy sweeps it some more.
Poor Mommy so busy, poor Daddy so sore.
Too busy to play, oh what a bore.
That Hair! That Hair! It's everywhere!

Hair! Hair! Hair!
Oh no! Oh my! Can you believe it?
There's hair in the toilet. Wouldn't you know it.
There's hair in the tub. There's so much to scrub.
There's hair in the sink. There's more than you think.
That Hair! That Hair! It's everywhere!

Hair! Hair! Hair!
Forget the hair! Forget the hair! Let's leave it there!
Let's go for a drive, away from the hair.
But wait, what's this? There's even hair there.
That Hair! That Hair! It's everywhere!

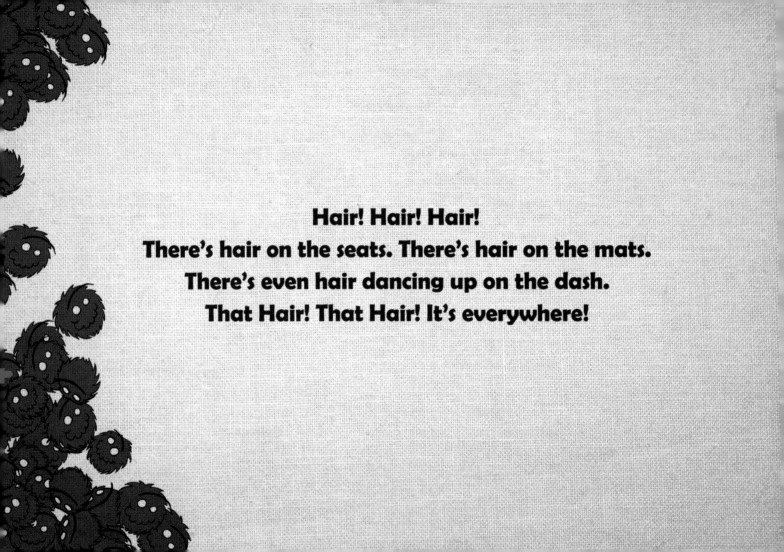

Hair! Hair! Hair!
There's hair on the seats. There's hair on the mats.
There's even hair dancing up on the dash.
That Hair! That Hair! It's everywhere!

Hair! Hair! Hair!
Forget it! Forget it! The hairs a prowlin'!
I'm hungry! I'm hungry! My tummy's a growlin'!
That Hair! That Hair! It's everywhere!

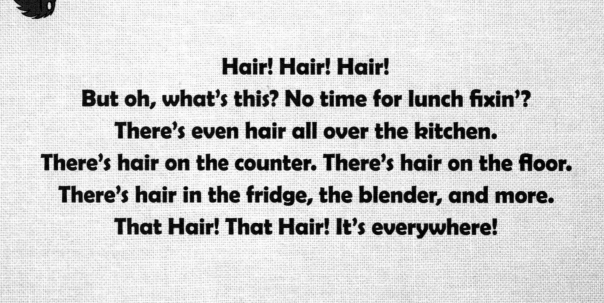

Hair! Hair! Hair!
But oh, what's this? No time for lunch fixin'?
There's even hair all over the kitchen.
There's hair on the counter. There's hair on the floor.
There's hair in the fridge, the blender, and more.
That Hair! That Hair! It's everywhere!

Hair! Hair! Hair!
Oh no! Indeed, I did have a hunch!
Can you believe it? There's hair in my lunch!
All of the brushin' and scoopin', won't free it!
This simply won't do, I refuse to eat it!
That Hair! That Hair! It's everywhere!

Hair! Hair! Hair!
I'm tired. I'm tired. I need to sleep.
I'm tired. So tired. Why weep and weep?
That Hair! That Hair! It's everywhere!

Hair! Hair! Hair!
Oh my! Oh my! What a surprise!
There's hair on my pillow. There's hair on my bed.
If I sleep here, I'm sure the hair...
Will bounce up on my head.
That Hair! That Hair! It's everywhere!

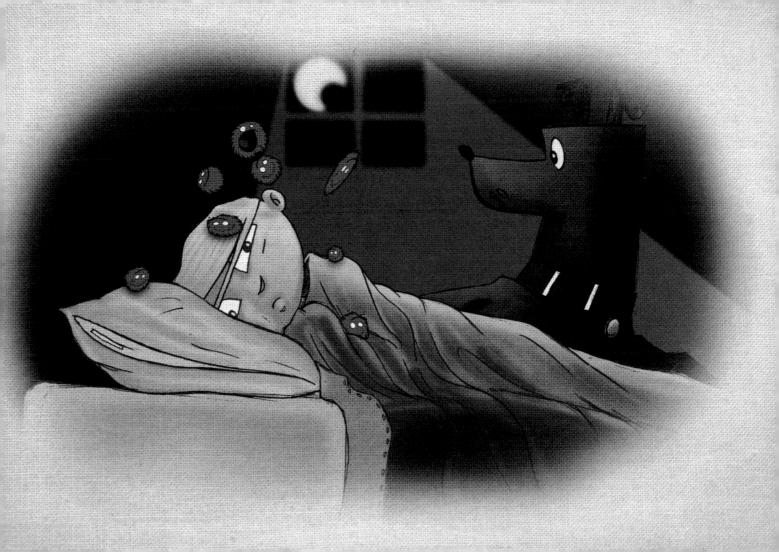

They told me my doggy wouldn't shed hair.
They're wrong by golly, they're wrong!
From front to back, from paw to head,
my doggy sheds and sheds.
From our house, to my clothes, to our car, it's a fact...
You may think I'm crazy; it's in my backpack.
Off to school I go, with hair, crayons, books, papers, and pens.
Hair everywhere, hair everywhere, it just never ends!
BUT....

No matter where you go, no matter what you do,
the hair will just fly, but this is nothing new.
No matter how you try and make the hair halt,
doggy hair grows and sheds, it's not your doggy's fault!

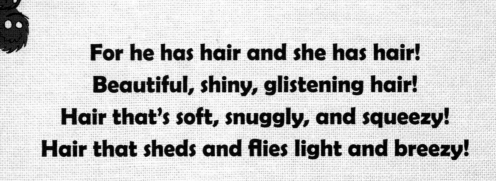

For he has hair and she has hair!
Beautiful, shiny, glistening hair!
Hair that's soft, snuggly, and squeezy!
Hair that sheds and flies light and breezy!

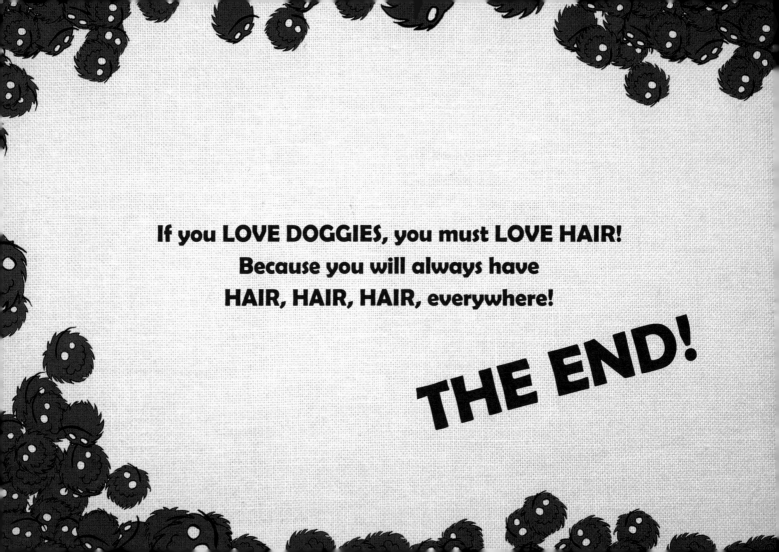

If you LOVE DOGGIES, you must LOVE HAIR!
Because you will always have
HAIR, HAIR, HAIR, everywhere!

THE END!

Meet Buster Posey (The HAPPY Lab!)

Born on October 17, 2010 (San Francisco Giants World Series Pennant Game)

Buster has Keratoconjunctivitis Sicca — Commonly known as Dry Eye Syndrome (DES). Buster has little to no tear production and is going blind. Buster needs three different eye drops administered three times per day or his eyes will crack. He will continue to have the eye drops administered for the duration of his life. The eye medication is very expensive and an on-going cost applied to "Buster's Slush Fund." Buster has regularly scheduled visits to the vet to prevent the continued development of ulcerated eyes and cataracts because of the long-term effects from prescription eye medications and his DES. DES is just one of many defects that affect animals.

Buster lives with the Robnetts in Sandy, Oregon. A stone's throw away from Mt. Hood. Melissa Robnett is Buster's master. Her studies are in Special Education and focused on specialized skills for individuals with special needs, including children. Melissa is the perfect master for Buster because of his DES. Her education, skills, and personal experiences with special needs individuals and children, brings an abundance of joy to Buster's personal needs. I feel ever blessed for the Robnetts.

I was the breeder who delivered Buster. Because of Buster's handicap, I launched Buster's Vision Nonprofit's campaign to save animals through the tools of a desperately needed education. Buster's Vision is a non-profit dedicated to provide the public with a positive, encouraging ANIMAL EDUCATION, promoting an awareness to protect the WELFARE OF ANIMALS, buyers and respectable breeders and to develop higher standards of ethical business practice and conduct.

Buster's Message To The Public:
Educate yourself prior to buying or adopting an animal. Animals are abandoned daily due to Lack of Education, Time & Money.
Thank you for reading my story.

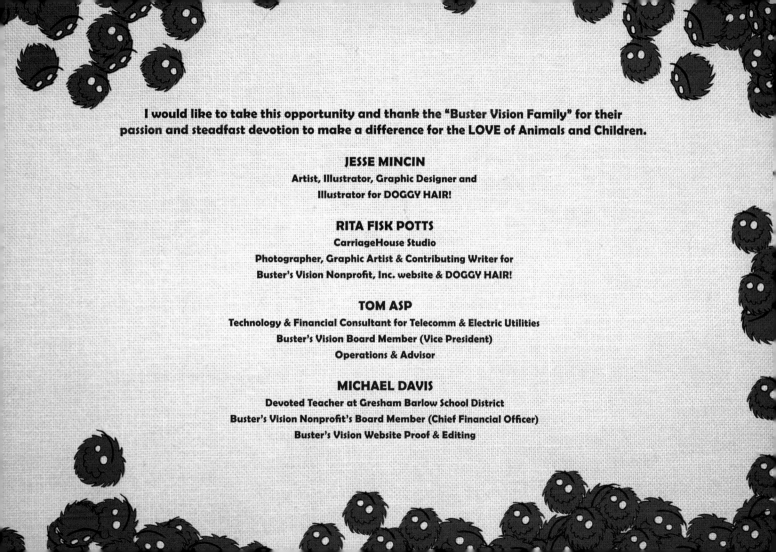

I would like to take this opportunity and thank the "Buster Vision Family" for their passion and steadfast devotion to make a difference for the LOVE of Animals and Children.

JESSE MINCIN
Artist, Illustrator, Graphic Designer and
Illustrator for DOGGY HAIR!

RITA FISK POTTS
CarriageHouse Studio
Photographer, Graphic Artist & Contributing Writer for
Buster's Vision Nonprofit, Inc. website & DOGGY HAIR!

TOM ASP
Technology & Financial Consultant for Telecomm & Electric Utilities
Buster's Vision Board Member (Vice President)
Operations & Advisor

MICHAEL DAVIS
Devoted Teacher at Gresham Barlow School District
Buster's Vision Nonprofit's Board Member (Chief Financial Officer)
Buster's Vision Website Proof & Editing

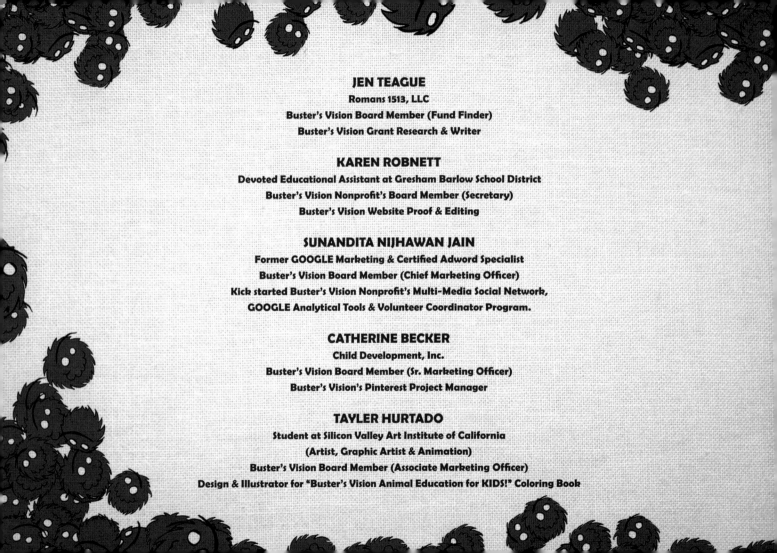

JEN TEAGUE
Romans 1513, LLC
Buster's Vision Board Member (Fund Finder)
Buster's Vision Grant Research & Writer

KAREN ROBNETT
Devoted Educational Assistant at Gresham Barlow School District
Buster's Vision Nonprofit's Board Member (Secretary)
Buster's Vision Website Proof & Editing

SUNANDITA NIJHAWAN JAIN
Former GOOGLE Marketing & Certified Adword Specialist
Buster's Vision Board Member (Chief Marketing Officer)
Kick started Buster's Vision Nonprofit's Multi-Media Social Network,
GOOGLE Analytical Tools & Volunteer Coordinator Program.

CATHERINE BECKER
Child Development, Inc.
Buster's Vision Board Member (Sr. Marketing Officer)
Buster's Vision's Pinterest Project Manager

TAYLER HURTADO
Student at Silicon Valley Art Institute of California
(Artist, Graphic Artist & Animation)
Buster's Vision Board Member (Associate Marketing Officer)
Design & Illustrator for "Buster's Vision Animal Education for KIDS!" Coloring Book

CODY FABSTEIN
Student at Silicon Valley Art Institute of California (Film, Videographer)
Buster's Vision Board Member (Associate Marketing Officer)
Co-Project Film/Videographer for Buster's Vision

MELISSA ROBNETT
Student at Western Oregon University (Special Education)
Project Manager for Buster's Corner (Blog)

JACOPONE AYALA
Student at Silicon Valley Art Institute of California (Film, Videographer)
Co-Project Film/Videographer for Buster's Vision

I would like to give special thanks to Vannessa Howe (Unit Director of the Levin Clubhouse of Boys and Girls Club of Silicon Valley)
for giving Buster's Vision that "Open Door Opportunity" to present "DOGGY HAIR!" and launch our first
"Buster's Vision Animal Education for KIDS!" presentation.

Buster's Vision encourages you to foster or adopt an animal today.
You can make a difference!

DOGGY HAIR!

Written by Bobbi Evenson
Illustrated by Jesse Mincin